Adventures in the DESERT

Rose Parkhurst

ISBN 978-1-68517-657-0 (paperback)
ISBN 978-1-68517-658-7 (digital)

Christian Faith Publishing
832 Park Avenue
Meadville, PA 16335
www.christianfaithpublishing.com

Printed in the United States of America

To Wounded Warriors.

A portion of the proceeds will be donated to charity.

School's out. Ruben and Alex are excited for another summer break with cousins Jonah and Austyn.

Let's get ready to pick them up at the Greyhound bus station.

There's Jonah and Austyn. Let's help with backpacks.

All four boys high-five and talk about food, family, friends, and adventures for the summer.

After dropping off backpacks, the boys are off to visit Nana and Tata.

Nana is making tamales and gives big hugs to Jonah and Austyn.

Tata is detailing his classic car to take the boys for a cruise after tamales.

The smell of homemade tortillas filled the air, and the boys are awake and excited to spend the day with their Nana. Nana is taking them to the Veteran's Hospital where she works and volunteers.

The gift shop is open; so Ruben and Alex say hi to a schoolteacher, Frances, who volunteers. Frances gives all the boys candy treats.

It's finally here! Uncle Milton's dude ranch for a week. Looks like our cousin Cash is loading horses for the rodeo tomorrow. Uncle Milton and Cash tell the boys to invite friends for a sunset BBQ and swimming. There are a lot of cousins and friends to invite, but Aunt Esther is making s'mores for the campfire, and the boys are excited.

What time is the rodeo today?

Our friend Lauren will be riding and competing in the rodeo with our cousin Scarlett. Let's watch the rodeo with Uncle Milton and Cash.

Lauren and her horse, Trinity, win the event.

I hope we get to see UFOs today…

All the boys are going to the observatory with cousin Jared today. It's a long trip, so the boys stop at Starbucks on the way.

Wow! Look at our solar system. I think I see a pyramid-shaped UFO.

The boys wake up to the smell of chorizo and have to get ready for golf with Tia Rose. Alex wants to drive the golf cart this time.

Tia Rose is so excited to play golf with Ruben, Alex, Jonah, and Austyn again.

Summer break is almost over…

Ruben has football practice in the Cherokee reservation with his friends Bobby and Patrick. The boys pack a lunch for the day. Bobby is the quarterback and calls for warm-ups. Ruben plays guard and starts conditioning. The team is excited for football season with Patrick as the starting linebacker.

After practice, the boys head over to the Pueblo Mission to say a prayer and give thanks. Nana and Tata were married at the Mission.

Today, Ruben and Alex are taking Jonah and Austyn to Tia Maria's barbershop for the goodbye party tomorrow. All the boys get shaved heads and look handsome.

Tia Maria makes tacos and quesadillas for lunch.

Summer break is over…

Nana is making homemade tortillas for the goodbye party. Tata has Ruben and Jonah cleaning the BBQ grill and patio while the younger boys Austyn and Alex are in the kitchen cutting up all the fruits and vegetables for salad and fajitas.

This will be the boys' last campfire together till next summer.

Everyone at the party gives thanks and wishes safe travel to Jonah and Austyn.

About the Author

Born in Tucson, Arizona, Rose grew up reading *Reader's Digest* with her dad. In school, she took communications and journalism, hoping to be a weather girl someday. Life had other plans. After two miscarriages and a failed adoption, Rose focused on a career dreaming about writing for children.

With the opportunity to babysit, volunteer, sponsor, and donate, she realized how important it is to pay it forward. This is her second children's book in a series of three showing the importance of faith, family, and friends.

CPSIA information can be obtained
at www.ICGtesting.com
Printed in the USA
JSHW030217231122
33718JS00005B/53